LYNNE RAE PERKINS

FRANK
AND
LUCKY

GET SCHOOLED

GREENWILLOW BOOKS
An Imprint of HarperCollinsPublishers

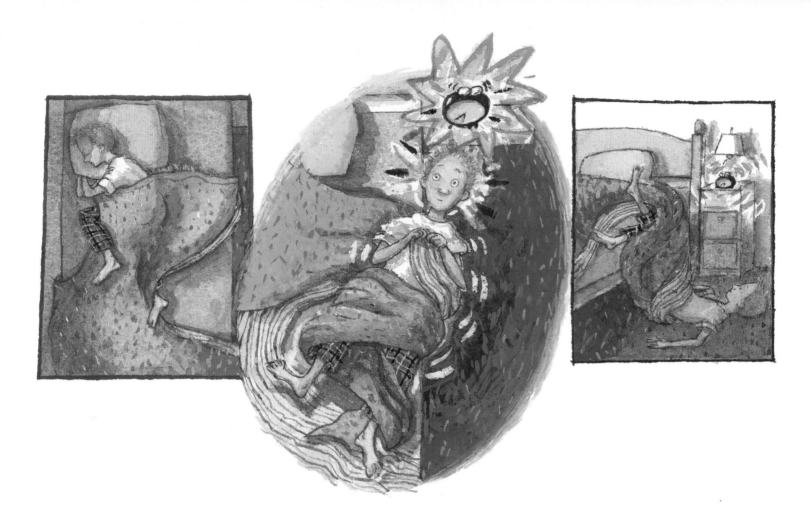

Frank and Lucky Get Schooled

Copyright © 2016 by Lynne Rae Perkins. All rights reserved. Manufactured in China. For information address HarperCollins Children's Books, a division of HarperCollins Publishers, 195 Broadway, New York, NY 10007. www.harpercollinschildrens.com

Pen and ink and watercolor paint were used to prepare the full-color art. The text type is Delima MT.

Library of Congress Cataloging-in-Publication Data
Perkins, Lynne Rae.
Frank and Lucky get schooled / by Lynne Rae Perkins.
  pages cm
"Greenwillow Books."
Summary: A boy and his dog learn about each other, go to school to learn more, then explore the world around them as they study science, geography and even foreign languages together.
ISBN 978-0-06-237345-8 (trade ed.)
[1. Learning—Fiction. 2. Dogs—Fiction. 3. Humorous stories.] I. Title.
PZ7.P4313Fr 2016 [E]—dc23 2015015559

16 17 18 19 20 SCP 10 9 8 7 6 5 4 3 2 1
First Edition

 Greenwillow Books

For true friends and scholars
of all species

One day when Frank could not win for losing, he got Lucky.

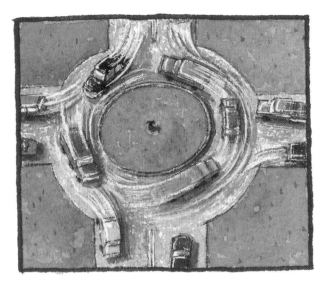  

And one day when Lucky was lost and found, he got Frank.

Both of them were just pups. They had a lot to learn.

First they learned about each other.

Then it was time to learn about other things. So off they went to school.

Lucky went to his school ten times. Frank went to his school thousands of times. Still, Lucky could always help Frank with his homework, because Lucky did a lot of learning on his own.

For example, Lucky was very interested in Science. Who isn't?

Science is when you wonder about something, so you observe it and ask questions about it and try to understand it.

Lucky wondered about ducks.

Can I catch it?

Can I eat it?

You like worms?
I like worms, too!

He wondered about squirrels and deer and bees and porcupines and little birds. He observed snow and rain, mud and grass, ponds and streams. He asked questions.

What is this stuff?

Does it feel good?

Is it my friend?

"beggar's-lice"
(*Hackelia virginiana*)

burdock

dog tick

When Lucky came home, he helped Frank learn about Botany, which is Science about plants, and Entomology, which is Science about bugs.

The time Lucky wondered about skunks, they learned about Chemistry, which is Science about what everything is made of, and how one kind of thing can change into another kind of thing.

Experiments are when you ask a question and then you try to find out the answer. If one experiment doesn't work, you try a different one.

No matter how experiments turn out, you always learn something.
Sometimes what you learn is Astronomy.

There's the Big Dipper. And see that star there, Lucky? That's called the Dog Star!

Can we go in the house yet?

No. Not yet.

Dog Star

It must be said that Lucky was not good at Taxonomy, the part of science that is about remembering the names of things. He was better at the experimenting part.

In Reading, he was best at the listening part. He could listen more than anyone else in the family. He could listen for hours, even when Frank wasn't reading aloud.

How much more could he listen? *How many* hours?

Wait a minute—aren't those Math questions?

Both Lucky and Frank loved Math. Math is puzzles. Math is *how much* and *how many*. Let's say a dog comes in from outside and gets one biscuit, but there are three people in the living room. How many more biscuits should the dog receive?

a) 2

b) A lot. Probably 5.

c) Maybe ∞

The dog should receive zero biscuits.

The answer is "c." The symbol ∞ means "infinity," which means that whatever is the biggest number you can think of, you can always add one and make an even bigger number. That is the number of biscuits Lucky was willing to eat.

Next question: Maybe it's shedding season.

Is the amount of hair a dog sheds in one week:

    a) > (more than)

    b) < (less than)

        or

    c) = (equal to)

the amount of hair the dog started out with?

The answer is "a) >." (More than. Much more than.)

How much hair does the dog have left?

The same amount as before. The dog keeps growing more hair. Which we know because of Science. Math and Science often go together.

When it's nighttime, how much of the bed is Lucky's, and how much is Frank's?

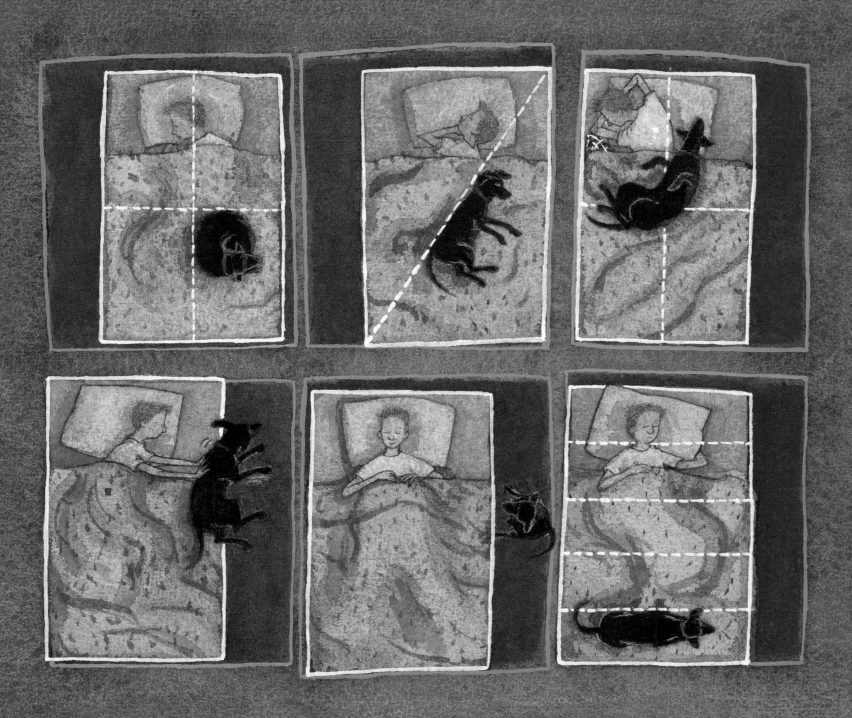

This is fractions and percentages. The answer changes throughout the night.

Frank has 2 legs. Each leg is 23" long.
Lucky has 4 legs. Each leg is 11" long.
Who has more fun?

There is no answer. We do not
have instruments precise enough
to measure the difference.

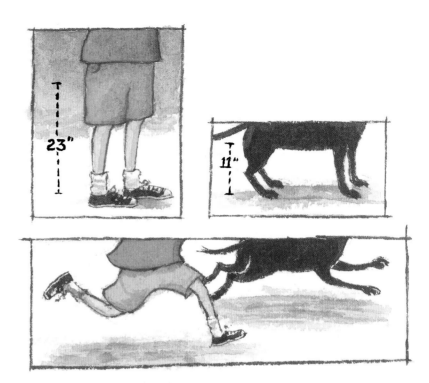

Okay, one more: If a chair is accidentally left
pulled out from the table at 8:30 in the morning,
how much cake will be left at 4:00 in the afternoon?

This is a *how much*
question, but it's not
a Math question. It's a
predicting-the-future question.
We won't know the answer
until someone comes home.

And then it will be a History
question.

Because History is what happened in the past. The olden days. Long, long ago. Or long ago. Or even not-so-long ago. These stories are History:

Long, long ago, all animals were wild. Dogs were the first animals who chose to be tamed by humans.

There are paintings in caves of people with their dogs.

Long ago, in Switzerland,
a dog named Barry found and
rescued more than forty people
who got lost in the mountain snows.

The hostel where he lived still keeps
one dog named Barry in his honor,
and there is a monument to him near
Paris, France.

And long ago, dogs pulling dogsleds
carried medicine to save people in
Nome, Alaska, from a deadly illness.

A dog named Balto kept his team on the trail
when the snow was so thick that the driver couldn't
see his hand in front of his face.

There is a statue of Balto in Central Park,
in New York City.

Not so long ago, a dog named Lucky jumped up onto a chair and ate an entire birthday cake that was on the table. At least, the evidence suggests that's what happened. Sometimes in History there are different versions of what really happened, depending on who is telling the story.

Cake? What cake?

There is a sculpture of Lucky, too. It's on Frank's dresser. Frank made it out of clay, in Art class.

In Art, Lucky helped by being the inspiration. The muse. And sometimes, the subject.

This kind of picture is called a Still Life. Because nothing is moving.

Here is an art lesson: every picture can be better with a dog in it. Or a cat.

If the picture has a dog AND a cat, people who look at it might feel that something exciting is about to happen. Their eyes will go back and forth between the cat and the dog. Making people's eyes move around to different parts of the picture is called Composition.

Making some parts look close while other parts look far away is called Perspective.

The part of the picture where the land and the sky come together is called the Horizon Line. If a dog is sitting at the Horizon Line, he will look like a Silhouette, which is the outline of an object filled in with a solid color, usually black.

Then you will have to go get him and bring him home. You will both be tired, and hungry.

You may decide to eat the Still Life.
That's what Frank and Lucky did.
The Art lesson was over. It was time
to get some sleep.

Because morning was one of their favorite times for Geography.

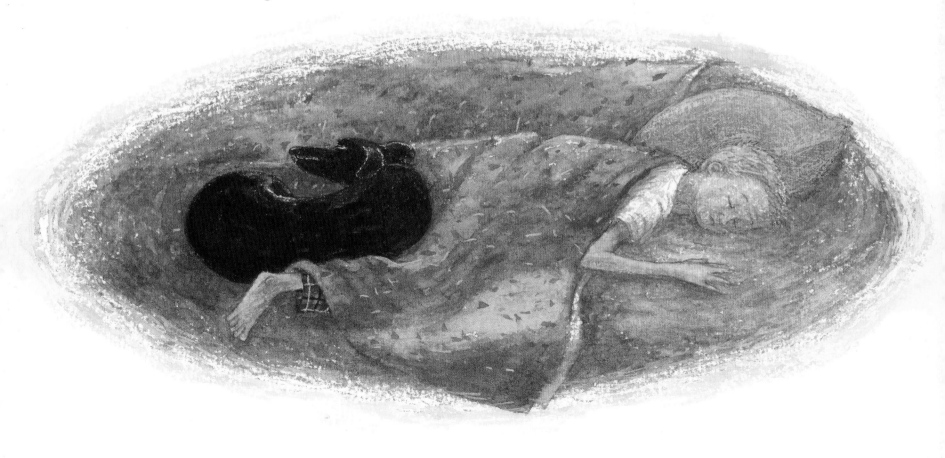

Geography is about our home, the Earth.

The whole Earth, and little pieces of it, and how the pieces fit together.
Also, who lives there.

This brings us to Maps.

A map is a picture that explains here and there, what and where. The picture
can be on paper or on a computer, or it can be an idea in your mind.

A map can explain how to get from here to there.

A map can tell how here is different from there. It can show how all the pieces of a place fit together. Geography and maps can lead to exploring and travel.

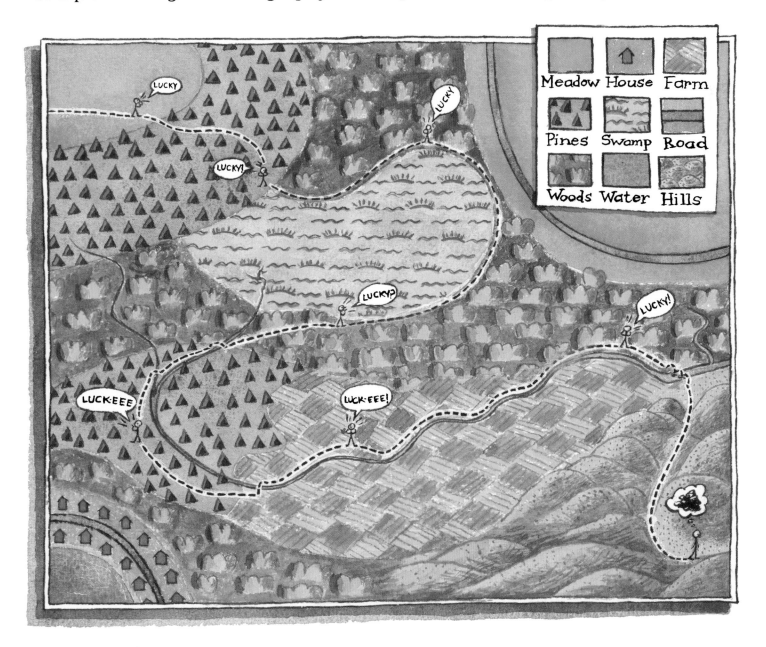

Which can lead to Foreign Languages. Frank was learning Spanish.

But he was very good at communicating with People, no matter what language they spoke. His specialty was Making Introductions.

His other specialty was Hospitality, which is making others feel welcome.

* We have some excellent Geography nearby. Shall we go look at it? Please??

Lucky never got tired of Geography. Neither did Frank. For one thing, it was always full of Science.

The Science was jam-packed with Art.

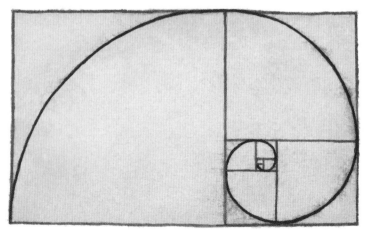

The Art, if you looked closely, had plenty of Math.

And the Math could tell Stories, even History.

Everything had a lot of everything else in it.

It would take a lot of time and exploring to learn how it all fit together.

How much time? Maybe ∞. Which was just right. Because

∞ + Frank

was Lucky's favorite number.

And the whole wide world with Lucky

was the subject Frank liked best.